VALENTINE

THE STORY OF

VALENTINE

by Wilma Pitchford Hays

Illustrated by Leonard Weisgard

Coward-McCann,
Inc. · New York

For
Two Graces

C. 2

IN a narrow street of Rome, four boys played
catch. Suddenly they heard the pounding of horses'
hoofs and the clatter of chariot wheels behind them.

"Jump! We'll be run over," shouted Octavian, the
tallest of the boys.

Octavian could feel the hot breath of the black
horses as the lead chariot thundered past him. The
horses shied. The wheels of the red and gold chariot
scraped against a corner of the building. The whip
flew from the hands of the charioteer as he stood with
his legs braced wide apart.

He shouted at the boys and leaped from his chariot. Before he could pick up his whip, the four boys ran. Around a corner and down another street they fled. They hid behind a high stone garden wall.

For several minutes they flattened themselves against the wall. Then Octavian leaned forward and peered down the street.

"No one's coming," he said.

The other boys gathered around him. Octavian ran a hand over his short black curls. His tunic was ripped. Beneath it, his bare brown legs were scratched. He was still breathing hard.

"We made that charioteer lose the race," he said.

"He should have known better," Antony said. "The street is no place for racing."

"Just the same, he was angry," Gaius said.

"What if he finds us?" said Cicero, the smallest of the boys. He was shaking. "We've been warned not to play in the streets."

"Where then?" Octavian asked. "We can't gather

in our own courtyards, unless we whisper. My little sister Agrippina takes a nap in the afternoon—and my mother, too."

"Mine, too," the other boys chorused.

"I guess there's nothing to do but go home and study our Greek," Antony said in disgust.

Behind them the boys heard a chuckle. They turned quickly and saw a stout man standing at an open gate in the garden wall. He wore a toga, the dress of a citizen of Rome. From a chain around his ample waist hung a small gold cross.

"Valentine," Octavian said. "You startled us."

. "I was studying here in my garden," the old priest said. "I heard you boys talking."

He smiled and held up a key.

"Don't worry again about where you will play. Come into my garden whenever you wish. There's room for your games beyond the olive trees. Your noise won't trouble me. Just call to me each day when you come to the gate. I'll unlock it for you."

9

For a moment the boys hesitated. Octavian could see into the garden. How green and cool it looked compared to the hot street. He wiped the sweat from his forehead with the back of his arm. He looked at the other boys. They too were staring longingly into the green garden, but none of them moved.

Octavian had spoken often to the kindly priest Valentine on the streets. But to go into his garden was another thing. Octavian had heard talk about the Christians. It was said that Emperor Claudius had issued a decree against them because he blamed the Christians for Rome's troubles.

Valentine went back into his garden. He turned to see if the boys were following.

"Come on," Octavian said in a low voice. "It's silly to be afraid of a good old man because he worships differently than we do."

Octavian hurried through the gate into the garden and the others followed.

As the heavy stone gate closed behind the boys,

they looked about. What a beautiful cool place this garden was. Rose vines climbed up the high stone walls. Flowers bloomed in neat borders along the paths. A small fountain of water sprayed a cool mist that felt good on the boys' hot faces. Nearby was a stone bench with books and paper and quill where Valentine had been studying. Against one of the walls was a small house where Valentine lived alone.

As the boys started toward the olive grove beyond, there was a sudden whir of wings overhead. A pigeon flew down, and lighted on Valentine's shoulder.

The old man touched the ash-colored head of the bird. "You're such a curious fellow, Smoky. You had to see who was visiting us?"

The boys clustered around Valentine and the pigeon. The bird cocked his head and looked down at them from his perch on the old man's shoulder. He stood first on one gray-pink foot, then the other. He made a cooing sound in Valentine's ear.

Octavian stepped nearer. The bird watched him from bright eyes and Octavian smiled.

"You are the very color of smoke," he said, "the light-gray cloud of smoke that comes from a bonfire of burning leaves. Smoky is a good name for you."

"He's so tame," said Antony. "He doesn't fly from us."

Valentine smiled and reached up his hand to stroke the pigeon.

"Smoky was only a little fellow when I found him in my garden with a broken wing. I cared for him until it healed. He has stayed close to me ever since. Sometimes he flies away for a short time but he always returns."

"Doesn't he ever get lost?" Cicero asked. "I wouldn't want to go far alone."

"He always knows his way home," Valentine said.

Smoky preened his feathers with his pearl-gray beak as if he was proud of himself but too modest to show his pride. Then he flew over to Valentine's work bench. Valentine followed.

All afternoon the boys played in the garden under the olive trees and at evening they went home.

13

"Goodbye," they called to Valentine as he let them out the gate. "Thank you for this wonderful place to play. We'll be back tomorrow."

Each day the boys came to the garden. Sometimes they played. Sometimes they helped Valentine care for his flowers. They dug along the paths where the plants had spread too wide. Smoky hopped along behind them and pecked at the fresh earth. He made cooing sounds of approval.

One afternoon Octavian stayed to finish a row after the other boys had left. He laughed when Smoky pulled a sprouted pea seed from a clod of earth Octavian held in his hand.

"You act as if I dig here just so you can fill your stomach," he said.

Nearby, Valentine was untangling a rose climber. He chuckled. "It is easy for us to think the world is run for our special benefit," he said.

Octavian looked up at the old man. How wise Valentine was. During the past weeks he had told the boys many stories. He seemed to know all that

had happened in the years gone by. He told them of the heroes of old, not only the great Roman heroes of whom Octavian had read in school, but others, too. Valentine knew stories of the Jewish leaders, Samson and David and Joseph. He knew stories of the wise men of the East, the Magi from Persia. He had told the boys of noble Greeks. And he told them of the one true God who loved and watched over all these people.

Octavian's dark brows drew together as he thought of the rumble of talk in the streets of Rome. Many people were afraid of anyone who believed in one loving God instead of the twelve stern gods of Rome.

Octavian didn't know that he looked troubled until he heard Valentine speak to him. "What is the matter, my son?"

Valentine came and sat down to rest on a bench beside Octavian. The boy, kneeling on the ground, looked up into the old man's face.

"I'm afraid for you," he said.

16

The old man did not answer. Octavian took hold of the bench with his muddy hand. "People are saying that Rome was powerful and strong when our people went regularly to the altars of the gods. Now they say we have grown careless. The gods are angry. People say that is why the sickness is spreading, why we lost a ship last week at sea. And they say—" The boy stopped and looked at Valentine as if he couldn't go on.

The old man waited.

"They say," Octavian almost whispered, "that we must kill those who do not believe in our Roman gods—or Rome will be destroyed."

Octavian felt the old man's fingers press into his shoulder.

"You are a good boy, Octavian," Valentine said gently. "Our country needs boys like you to grow up to be brave-thinking men. I pray the one true God that you will help Rome to trust people's differences and be fair to all."

The boy looked at Valentine's face lifted toward the sky. The goodness and kindness of the old man seemed almost like a light. A tingle went along Octavian's spine. His heart filled with a strange new wonder.

The sun went down behind the garden wall. A chill breeze reminded Octavian that it was time to go home, before his mother worried. He left Valentine praying and went out the garden gate.

As he started along the shadowed street, a small figure moved out from against the garden wall.

"Octavian," a little girl's voice called.

"Agrippina," Octavian cried. "What are you doing here? You know you are never allowed outside our courtyard."

"If your own sister can't warn you, then who can?" she said.

Octavian saw that Agrippina was bareheaded. Her dark curls hung loose to her shoulders. She hadn't even put a wrap over the straight white dress she wore.

"Warn me of what?" he said.

"I heard Mother and Father talking," Agrippina whispered. "Today Emperor Claudius sent his soldiers to arrest all those who do not worship Roman gods. I was afraid his soldiers might come here for the priest Valentine and find you, and take you to prison, too."

Octavian looked down at his sister. She was only

eight years old. She was frightened by the dusk and the strange streets, yet she had come for him. He took her hand. "Let's hurry home," he said gently. "I have just been talking to Valentine. He is such a good man. Emperor Claudius can't mean to arrest him."

That night Octavian found it hard to sleep. He tossed on his low couch. Twice he thought he heard the clank of soldiers' swords. But when he sat up and listened, he could hear only the clatter of horses' hoofs in the street outside. Perhaps soldiers were riding home late from the gladiator fights.

The next morning he was up early. He hurried to the gate in the garden wall.

"Valentine," he called. "It is Octavian. Unlock the gate, please."

There was no answer. He listened for sound of the old man's footsteps, but there was no sound. Never had there been such quiet inside the garden walls. Octavian's heart began to thump.

Perhaps the old man was still sleeping.

"Valentine," Octavian called again. "Please let me in."

Behind him in the street he heard the other boys coming. He called to them. "Valentine does not answer this morning. The gate is locked."

"Then all the talk is true," said Antony. "The soldiers have come for him."

"What shall we do?" Gaius asked.

"I think we should go home as fast as we can," Cicero said, looking fearfully about.

Octavian could feel the hot blood pounding in his temples so that his olive skin grew warm. "We are four Romans," he said, "each named for great men of our country. I don't think we should run away until we know what has happened to our friend Valentine. Maybe we can help him."

"What can we do against the soldiers of Rome?" asked Antony.

"We are only boys," Cicero said, "even if we are Romans."

Suddenly overhead came a whir of wings. The boys looked up. A pigeon circled over them and lighted on the stone pillar of the gate.

"It is Smoky," Octavian cried. "Do you think he has been with Valentine? If only he could tell us."

The pigeon shifted his gray-pink feet. There was a soft clanking sound against the stone gate. "Coo, coo," Smoky said as he turned about.

"Look, there on his leg," Octavian cried. "There's a key and a bit of paper. It must be from Valentine. He has sent us the key to the garden."

The boys rushed forward. Octavian was the tallest but he could not quite reach the pigeon. "Lift me a little," he called to the other boys. They gathered around him and lifted until he touched Smoky.

He fixed the legs of the pigeon carefully between his fingers as he had seen Valentine do. His other hand moved over Smoky gently. A little shock went through him as he felt the hard swift beating of the bird's heart against the palm of his hand.

Then he stood on the ground with the pigeon in his hands. The other boys ringed about them. How strong Smoky's wings and breast were. His beak was open a little. He watched the boys with bright eyes.

"Antony, you take the key and paper from his leg," Octavian said. "Be careful."

When Antony had the scrap of paper and key in his hand, Octavian loosened his hold on Smoky. He felt the small claws press hard against his fingers as the pigeon took off into the sky.

"He's flying toward the great square of Rome," Octavian said. "The prison is there. Do you think that means Valentine is in prison?"

The boys nodded. Antony began to unroll the paper and the others looked over his shoulder. In Valentine's fine, careful letters was written:

Here is the key to open my garden gate for you. Octavian, care for the key until I return.

Love from your Valentine

The boys ran to the gate. Octavian turned the key in the lock and the gate opened. The boys hurried inside, slamming the gate behind them. Then they stood still.

They looked at the empty bench where Valentine wrote, and at the closed windows of his little house.

"He told such good stories," Antony said.

"And drew little pictures to go with them," Gaius whispered.

"It's too still in here. It scares me," Cicero said.

Octavian swallowed a lump in his throat. The goodness and love of the old man seemed everywhere. Octavian could feel it in the touch of the sun on his face. It was in the feel of the grass, soft under his sandals.

"Valentine sent us the key so we could have a safe place to play," he said at last. "Even in prison he thinks of others. We will come here and care for his garden. Perhaps later we can find some way to help him."

Each day the boys came to the garden. Octavian always came first and slipped inside. He let each boy in quietly as he arrived.

They were careful not to shout within the walls. This was their secret place. They did not want anyone to stop their coming here. Sometimes they played games under the olive trees. But more often they found work to do.

"I didn't know there could be so many things to do in a garden," Antony said. He was raking fallen leaves.

"We can't burn those," Cicero said. "Someone might see the flames."

"Anyway, it isn't safe to start a fire in here," said Gaius.

"We'll pile the leaves against a corner wall and cover them with forked sticks," Octavian decided. "Except those we need to mulch the divine pinks and the herb bed. Valentine was very particular about the divine flower and his herbs."

The boys were carrying leaves when they heard a whir of wings. They dropped their leaves and for a moment forgot to be careful. "Smoky," they cried.

The pigeon fluttered down to the path and strutted back and forth as if he knew what an important visitor he was.

"Look, on his leg, a scrap of paper," Antony shouted.

"He's brought us news of Valentine," Octavian said. "Smoky, come here," he coaxed.

"Coo, coo," the pigeon said. He flew low over the ground, stopping just out of reach and pecking at the dry earth. He lifted his head and turned it a little to one side.

Octavian laughed. "He's asking for a pea. Smoky, you're trying to bribe us."

With his rake, Octavian turned over the dried pea vines. At once Smoky flew to him and began to eat the seeds. Octavian took the note from his leg. He read aloud to the other boys.

My dear young friends:

I am well treated here. I have a couch to sleep upon and food to eat. The prison keeper has been kind to me. He lets me have paper and a quill with which to write. But I miss my reading. How I wish I might have one of my rolls of books

Octavian stopped as if an idea had come suddenly into his head.

"Maybe Smoky could take one back," Gaius said.

"A rolled book is much too heavy for him," Antony said.

Octavian's heart beat hard. He knew the Book Valentine loved most. He had often seen Valentine lift it from the shelf in his study. He had watched Valentine unroll the Book carefully as he read. If only he could take the Book to Valentine in prison.

"Come, wake up," the boys were saying. "What else does Valentine say?"

Octavian began to read again.

32

My keeper has a little daughter about your age. Her name is Julia and she is blind. I used to watch her walk in the courtyard. Then one day she heard Smoky cooing from the stone sill of my prison window. She came nearer to hear Smoky and I spoke to her.

I have told Julia about you, my little friends. She couldn't understand how Smoky knows the way to go from this prison to the garden with my messages for you. I tell her it is simple. Whenever he is let free, he goes to one of the two places where he feels at home, to me or to the garden we love.

For a long time after Octavian finished reading, he felt the excited beating of his heart. If only he could get the Book to Valentine. His days in prison would not seem so long if he could read. Valentine had done so much for him. Now he wanted to help his old friend.

33

Octavian was still thinking of this when he and the others left the garden. Then, on the way home, he knew what he must do. He slipped back and unlocked the gate. He went to the small house and took the rolled Book from the study shelf. He placed it carefully under his toga, and drew his girdle tightly about him to hold the roll securely.

He didn't want to tell anyone where he was going. It was not safe for anyone to know he carried the Book about the one true God. That night as he lay on his couch, he remembered that the boys would come here to find him in the morning if he was not at the garden gate. He left his couch and went to his little sister's sleeping room.

"Agrippina," he said softly. "Are you asleep?"

She sat up quickly. He could see her dark hair and small white figure in the moonlight.

"You frightened me, Octavian," she whispered.

He came over to her bed and pressed the key to Valentine's garden into her hand.

34

"Tomorrow, when Antony and Cicero and Gaius come here, give them this key," he whispered. "Say that I cannot come to the garden today. I will come the next morning and I will have something to tell them."

He saw her small hand close tightly on the key. "Octavian, you are going to do something foolish," she whispered. "I always know when you are trying to keep something from me."

"It is not foolish to help as good a man as Valentine," Octavian said before he could think.

Suddenly his little sister was out of bed and holding his arm tightly. He could feel her trembling.

"You are more foolish than I thought. What are you going to do?"

"Shh," he said. "You will have everyone awake. I promise you I will be careful. I know the way to the prison."

"But you have never gone alone as far as the great square of Rome," Agrippina said.

36

"Every year at the feast of Saturnalia, I go with father to worship at the temple," Octavian said. "The prison is directly across the square. I have seen it many times.

"Promise you will not say a word to anyone, and I will bring you a doll. The prettiest doll I can find. I have been saving my coins to buy gifts for the feast of Saturnalia."

Agrippina hesitated. Octavian knew how she loved her dolls. He waited. Slowly she climbed back onto her couch.

"Promise me you will be careful, Octavian," she said. ". . . And pick the doll with the prettiest face."

Early the next morning Octavian left his home. He couldn't lose his way because many other people were traveling the dusty roads toward the Sacred Way which led to the Forum. Here in the great square of Rome were all the temples of the gods, the prison, and the shops. Octavian felt excited as he pushed among the crowds toward the city. At last he

37

came into the great square with its brightly deco-
rated stalls of weavers and jewel merchants and all
kinds of shops.

"Come, come," men's voices called loudly. "Buy
here your gifts for Saturnalia."

"Buy here. Buy here," a thin high voice called.
"Buy holly and greens. Make your home beautiful
to please our god Saturn."

All about Octavian the shouts were so loud that
he didn't know what to do first. Should he buy
Agrippina's doll? No, he had better do that on his
way home. First he must go to the prison.

As he walked through the market place, the de-
licious smells of food were too much for him. He
was so empty that he must buy something to eat. He
stood before the rows of market stalls. There hung
young pigs for roasting. Geese for stuffing. Figs for
pies. Dates from Africa. Jugs of wine and of goat's
milk.

"Buy! Buy here for the feast of Saturnalia," voices
shouted.

Octavian's mouth watered as he thought of the good things to come for the feast only a few days away. But he was hungry now. Then he saw the bakery with its shelves of hot round buns sprinkled with raisins and honey. He bought a fat bun, warm from the oven, and munched it as he walked along.

When he reached the prison gate, Octavian saw the guard. He had not thought of a guard. He stood across the street watching. How could he make his way inside the wall and find the barred window of Valentine's cell?

The guard clanked his sword. The sun glittered on his helmet as he opened the gate to let an official come out. As the gate opened, Octavian saw a young girl. She was walking in the courtyard. Julia, he thought. His heart beat hard.

He went up to the guard. "May I go in? I wish to see Julia, the prison keeper's daughter."

The guard looked at him and frowned. Octavian stood straight and tall and tried to remember that he wore the toga of a full citizen of Rome, even if it was crimson bordered to show that he was not yet a man.

The guard began to close the heavy gate.

"Julia," Octavian called.

"Who is it?" the girl answered.

Octavian could feel the fearful beat of his heart. What if she said she did not know him? He must get inside and tell her why he had come.

"I—I had a note from Smoky," he said.

He saw the girl stop. She must have guessed that he was trying to tell her something, because she spoke to the guard.

"Let the boy in," she said.

The guard stood aside and Octavian went into the courtyard.

"Julia," he said softly. "I am Octavian, Valentine's friend. Will you help me?"

She ran toward the sound of his voice, and stopped directly in front of him.

41

"I can hardly believe you do not see," he said in a wondering voice.

Julia smiled. She had soft brown hair that fluffed about her shoulders. She was only a little larger than Agrippina. Suddenly Octavian felt at home with her. He told her why he had come.

"If you will show me Valentine's window," he said, "I can reach the Book up to him."

Julia shook her head. "His window opens on the inner court," she said. "You could not go in there."

Octavian's heart sank. He had come all this way. Now he could not even speak to his friend. Worst of all, Valentine would not have his Book.

"He wants this Book so much," Octavian said. "There must be a way."

Julia seemed to be listening to tell if anyone was near.

"I know," she said softly. "My father says Valentine is a good and learned man. My father takes me with him to visit Valentine so I may learn from him. I have never been able to read for myself."

43

She stopped. Octavian heard the longing in her voice. His heart moved.

"I will take the Book to him," Julia said. "Give it to me. I will hide it in my skirt."

Carefully Octavian untied the rolled Book from under his toga. He put in into Julia's hand and she pulled a fold of her full skirt about to cover it.

"Take great care," Octavian said. "It is Valentine's favorite book."

"Does it tell of the one true God?" Julia asked softly.

Octavian looked at her. Then Valentine had told her, too, of the one God. She dared to speak of Him even inside these prison walls.

"You can trust me," Julia said. "Even as I trust you. Valentine has told me how thoughtful and brave you are. He says some day you will grow up to be a leader in the government of Rome. And you will speak, then, for love and fair treatment toward all men."

Octavian could feel the throbbing in his temples.

"I will," he said. "And you were right about the Book."

Julia's fingers closed more tightly on the Book. "Do you believe in the one true God?"

"I do not know," Octavian said.

Above the prison walls, he could see the dome of the temple of the lifeless god Saturn. Beyond that was the temple of Jupiter. Across the square was the temple to Juno. Behind him were temples to Venus and Mars and all the others of the twelve gods he had been taught to worship. One must be careful, because these gods could be jealous and angry. But Valentine spoke of a God of love who cared for all people, even those who were not Romans. It was very puzzling.

"I have seen Valentine lift his face to the sky," Octavian said. "I have seen the light that comes in his eyes when he speaks to his God. Then—then I almost—"

"*I believe*," Julia said. "And Valentine says that Faith is a powerful medicine." She leaned forward.

45

"Do you know what I ask for the feast of Saturnalia?"

"A doll?" Octavian guessed, remembering the one he had promised his sister.

Julia shook her head. "I pray to see," she said. "I pray each night and morning to the one true God for the gift of sight."

Octavian looked into the small girl's face. It seemed to be so full of hope and happiness that it was almost like a light.

His heart began to pound. A tingle went along his spine. He felt the same excitement that had come over him in the garden when he watched Valentine lift his face and pray.

Octavian found himself saying, "I pray for you, too. Oh, the one true God, give Julia sight."

When he understood what he had done, he grew even more excited. He was a Roman. Yet he had prayed to the one God of his friend Valentine.

He was trembling and strangely happy as he said goodbye to Julia and left the courtyard.

The next morning Octavian felt a chill east wind blowing from the River Tiber. The air coming into the family living room was damp. Perhaps the other boys wouldn't go to the garden today, he thought. He wanted very much to go. He hoped Smoky might bring a note from Valentine telling that the Book had reached him safely.

Agrippina came into the room, hugging the doll

48

Octavian had brought her. He spoke to her. "When you gave Antony the key, did you say I would have something to tell him and the others today?"

"Yes," Agrippina said. "They were so curious. They asked and asked, but I would not say where you had gone."

Octavian grinned. "Then they'll be in the garden even if it is cloudy," he said.

49

As he tried to cross the narrow street, he had to dodge galloping horses pulling a chariot. He saw people scatter and heard shouts of anger. He thought of that day, months ago, when he and Antony and Gaius and Cicero had run from an angry charioteer. Valentine had invited them to play in his garden. How different life was now because he had become a friend of Valentine.

He heard Antony calling to him. "Hurry, we're here ahead of you."

He met the other boys at the garden gate and they went inside. "Where were you yesterday? Tell us what happened," they cried.

Octavian told them of taking the Book, of his trip through the Forum and into the prison yard. He told of Julia, even of her prayer for sight.

"Do you think she really took the Book to Valentine?" Antony said.

"She'd be afraid," said Cicero. "What if a guard caught her with such a book?"

"Suppose she gave it to a guard and told him that *you* brought it?" Gaius said. "You'll be arrested. Already they may be coming for you."

Suddenly there was a whir of wings overhead.

"Smoky!" the boys called. "Smoky's here again."

The pigeon fluttered above them and lighted on Octavian's shoulder as if he knew the ground was cold today and wanted a warmer spot on which to perch. Octavian took the paper from around the bird's leg. He read aloud.

My dear young friends:
    I would not have asked you to take such a risk, but I thank you, Octavian, from the bottom of my heart for my Book.
    You will hardly be able to believe the thing that happened when it came. Julia brought it to me hidden in her skirt. When we were alone, she took it out and handed it to me. I was so happy when I saw it that I cried out, "Thank God!"

With the Book in my hands, I touched her head. She began to laugh and cry together.

"I can see," she kept saying. "I can see you, Valentine. I see the Book in your hand. I see the cross at your waist. Oh, it is so wonderful— wonderful to see!"

I am still a little shaky from the miracle of it, so I shall not write more tonight. But you can see, Octavian, what your journey with the Book has helped to bring about.

Love from your Valentine—

Octavian stood with the paper in his hands. He was a Roman. He must not cry, but his heart kept swelling and swelling. Julia can see. Julia can see.

"What do you suppose made such a miracle happen?" Antony said at last.

"Yes," Gaius said, "what?"

"I want to go home," Cicero whimpered, looking about fearfully. "It's cold. Besides—"

He hurried from the garden. Antony and Gaius walked slowly after him, whispering together. Octavian still stood with the paper in his hand and Smoky on his shoulder. His dark eyebrows drew together and his face was thoughtful.

"Smoky, you dropped into this garden with a broken wing. Now you are healed and carry messages from Valentine to us.

"Julia met Valentine in prison. Now she can see."

"Coo, coo," the pigeon said into Octavian's ear. The boy reached up and put his hand about the bird's soft body.

"Even I am changed in my heart," he said softly. "I no longer wish to be a charioteer and race in the arena. I want to grow up to be the kind of man Valentine wants me to be. I'll be a leader in my country and speak out for love and fairness toward all men."

"Coo, coo," Smoky said again.

And Octavian felt that the pigeon understood.

Valentine was a real person, one of the first Romans to believe in one God of love rather than the twelve stern gods of Rome. He loved children. We are told that even in prison, he cured the prison keeper's little daughter of blindness.

I wondered about the children who played in Valentine's garden and listened to his stories and petted his carrier pigeon. Did they learn of God from Valentine? And when he was sent to prison, how did they feel? Were they afraid, or did they want to help Valentine?

Then I imagined and wrote this story of Octavian, the Roman boy who undertook the dangerous task of getting into the prison to deliver to Valentine the Book about the one God—and of Julia, the little blind girl who helped him.

Years later, after most of the people of Rome had come to believe in one God, they wished to honor Valentine. His birthday, February fourteenth, came the day before the old Roman celebration Lupercalia, in honor of the "wolf destroyer" who had saved Rome from many dangerous packs of wild wolves. The people decided to change the name of this celebration to St. Valentine's Day. Now, on this day, we send messages to our friends as Valentine did long ago.